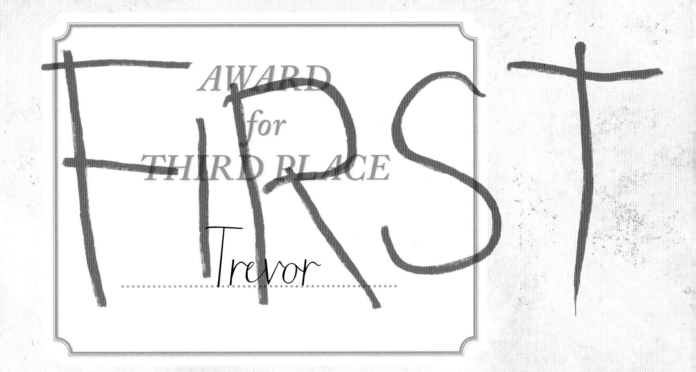

FIRST

AWARD
for
THIRD PLACE

Trevor

For the girl who cried silver tears.

Scholastic Canada Ltd.
604 King Street West, Toronto, Ontario M5V 1E1, Canada

Scholastic Inc.
557 Broadway, New York, NY 10012, USA

Scholastic Australia Pty Limited
PO Box 579, Gosford, NSW 2250, Australia

Scholastic New Zealand Limited
Private Bag 94407, Botany, Manukau 2163, New Zealand

Scholastic Children's Books
Euston House, 24 Eversholt Street, London NW1 1DB, UK

www.scholastic.ca

The artwork in this book is acrylic (with pens and pencils) on watercolour paper.

Library and Archives Canada Cataloguing in Publication

Blabey, Aaron, author, illustrator
Pig the winner / Aaron Blabey.
ISBN 978-1-4431-4891-7 (bound)
I. Title.
PZ10.3.B519Pw 2016   j823'.92   C2015-908299-4

First published by Scholastic Australia in 2016.
This edition published in Canada by Scholastic Canada Ltd. in 2016.

6 5 4 3 2 1   Printed in Malaysia 108   16 17 18 19 20

PIG the WINNER PUG

Aaron Blabey

Scholastic Canada Ltd.
Toronto New York London Auckland Sydney
Mexico City New Delhi Hong Kong Buenos Aires

Pig was a Pug
and I'm sorry to say,
if he didn't come first
it would ruin his day.

Yes, Pig was a winner.
He just HAD to win.
And nothing would stop him.
Oh, where to begin?

Believe it or not,
he was quite hard to beat.

And the reason was simple . . .

Yes, Pig was a cheat.

But if he DID lose,
he'd throw a big fit.
He'd scream and he'd cry
and he just wouldn't quit.

He'd sob and he'd sulk,
with a quivering chin,
till you gave up and said to him,
"OK. You win."

But as soon as you said it,
he'd clap and he'd stamp,
and he'd rub it in loudly
that HE was the champ.

Trevor would say to him,
"Let's just have fun."
But Pig would reply —

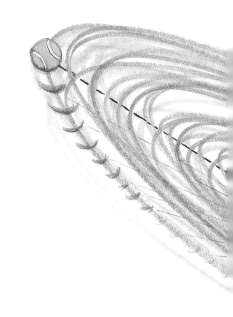

"It ain't fun till I've WON!"

So one night at supper,
Pig shouted with glee,
"Who can eat faster?
I bet that it's ME!"

Trevor said shyly,
"I don't want to race."
But Pig had yelled,

"GO!"

and was stuffing his face.

He wolfed down his dog food.
He gobbled his kibble.
His face was awash
with biscuits and dribble.

He chomped up three sausages —
all of them whoppers!
Then he munched through his doggie treats,
gnashing his choppers.

He swallowed it all in a minute or less.

But something went wrong.

Do you know?
Can you guess?

Because he was busy
stuffing his hole,
Pig didn't notice . . .

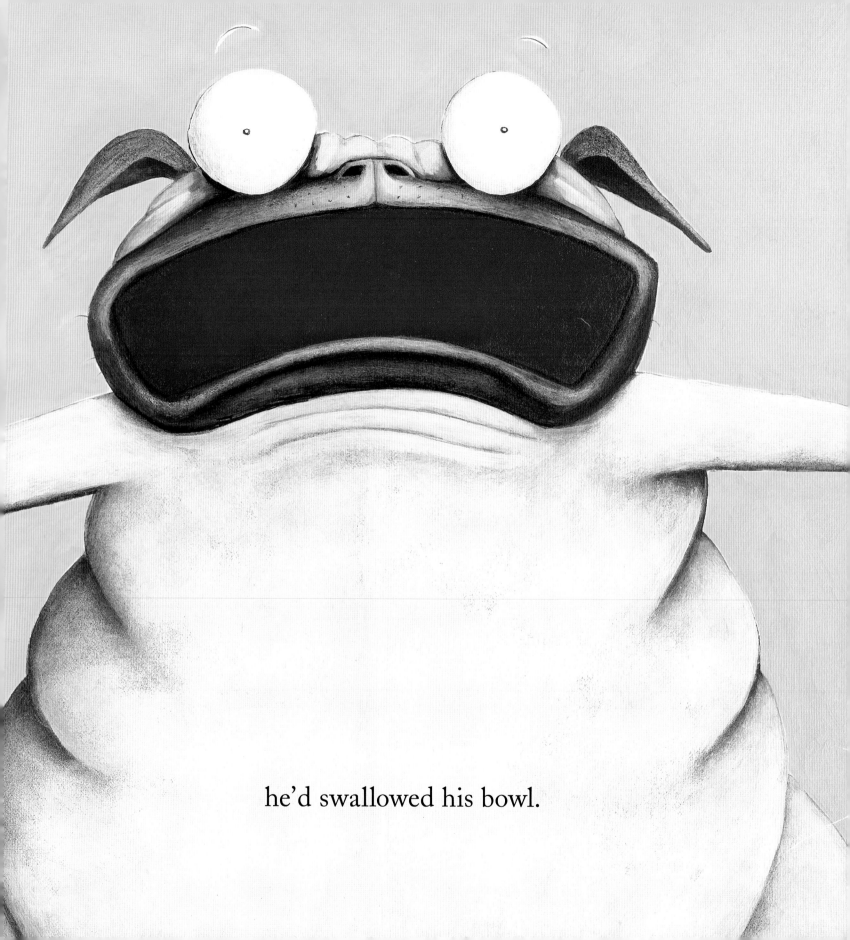

he'd swallowed his bowl.

Lucky for Pig,
Trevor knew what to do.
He squeezed out the bowl
before Pig could turn blue.

But Pig didn't thank him!
He just said,

"I WIN!"

Then the bowl bounced right back . . .

. . . and knocked Pig in the bin.

These days it's different,
I'm happy to say.
Pig's not the winner
each time that they play.

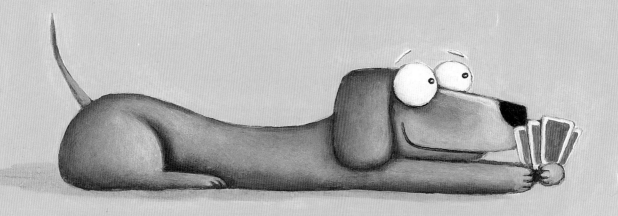

He plays to have fun,
and his tantrums have ceased.
Yes, Trevor can win now!

Well, sometimes, at least.

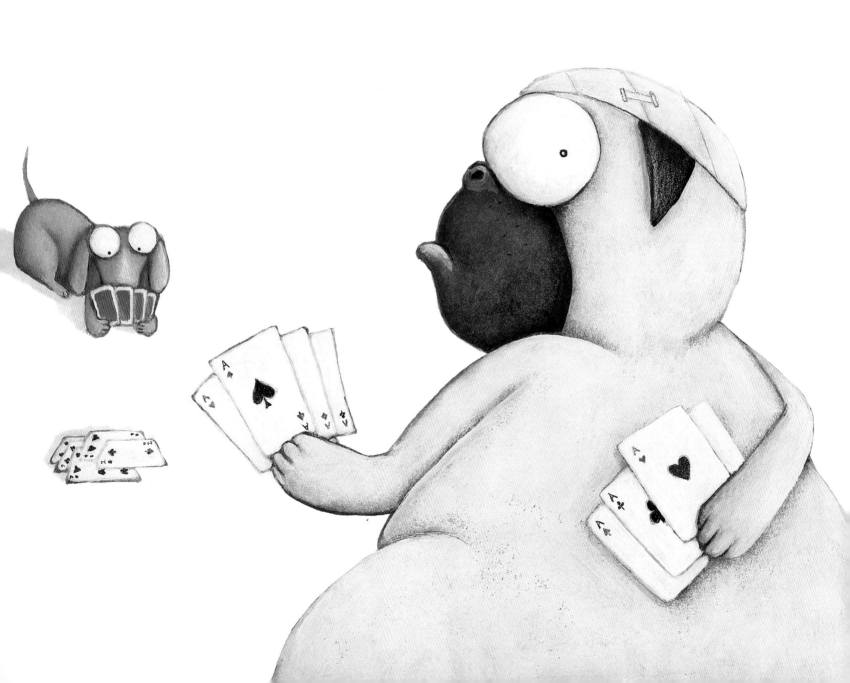